The Eric Carle Museum of Picture Book Art was built to celebrate the art that we are first exposed to as children. Located in Amherst, Massachusetts, the 40,000-square-foot museum is the first in this country devoted to national and international picture book art.

To find out more about the Eric Carle Museum of Picture Book Art, please visit www.carlemuseum.org.

To find out more about Eric Carle and his books and products, please visit eric-carle.com.

Henry Holt and Company, LLC
Publishers since 1866
175 Fifth Avenue, New York, New York 10010
mackids.com

Library of Congress Cataloging-in-Publication Data
Martin, Bill, 1916–2004
Polar bear, polar bear, what do you hear? / by Bill Martin Jr;
Pictures by Eric Carle.
Summary: Zoo animals from polar bear to walrus make their distinctive sounds for each other, while children imitate the sounds for the zookeeper.
ISBN 978-0-8050-9066-6
[1. Animal sounds—Fiction. 2. Zoo animals—Fiction. 3. Stories in rhyme.]
I. Carle, Eric, ill. II. Title.
PZ8.3.M4113Po   1991   [E]—dc20   91-13322

First published in 1991 by Henry Holt and Company
Larger-format book edition with audio CD—2011

Printed in July 2011 in China by South China Printing Company Ltd.,
Dongguan City, Guangdong Province.
10 9 8 7 6 5 4 3 2 1

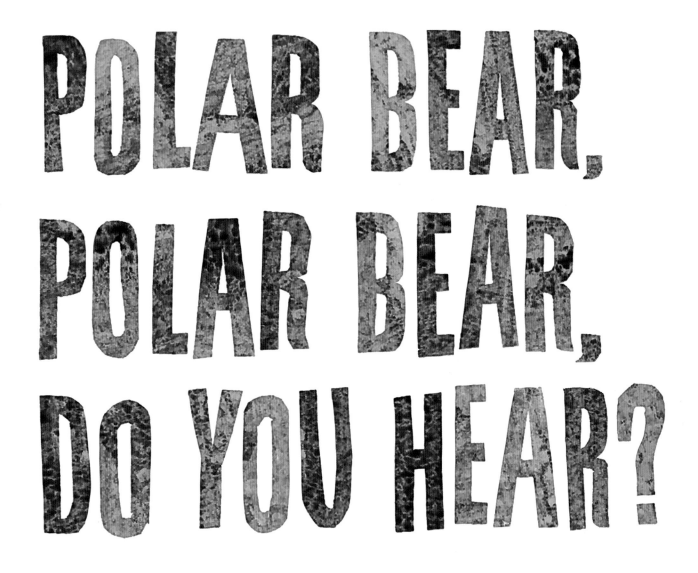

POLAR BEAR, POLAR BEAR, DO YOU HEAR?

By Bill Martin Jr
Pictures by Eric Carle

Henry Holt and Company · New York

Polar Bear, Polar Bear,
what do you hear?

I hear a lion
roaring in my ear.

Lion, Lion,
what do you hear?

I hear a hippopotamus
snorting in my ear.

Hippopotamus, Hippopotamus,
what do you hear?

I hear a flamingo
fluting in my ear.

Flamingo, Flamingo,
what do you hear?

I hear a zebra
braying in my ear.

Zebra, Zebra,
what do you hear?

I hear a boa constrictor
hissing in my ear.

Boa Constrictor, Boa Constrictor,
what do you hear?

I hear an elephant
trumpeting in my ear.

Elephant, Elephant,
what do you hear?

I hear a leopard
snarling in my ear.

Leopard, Leopard,
what do you hear?

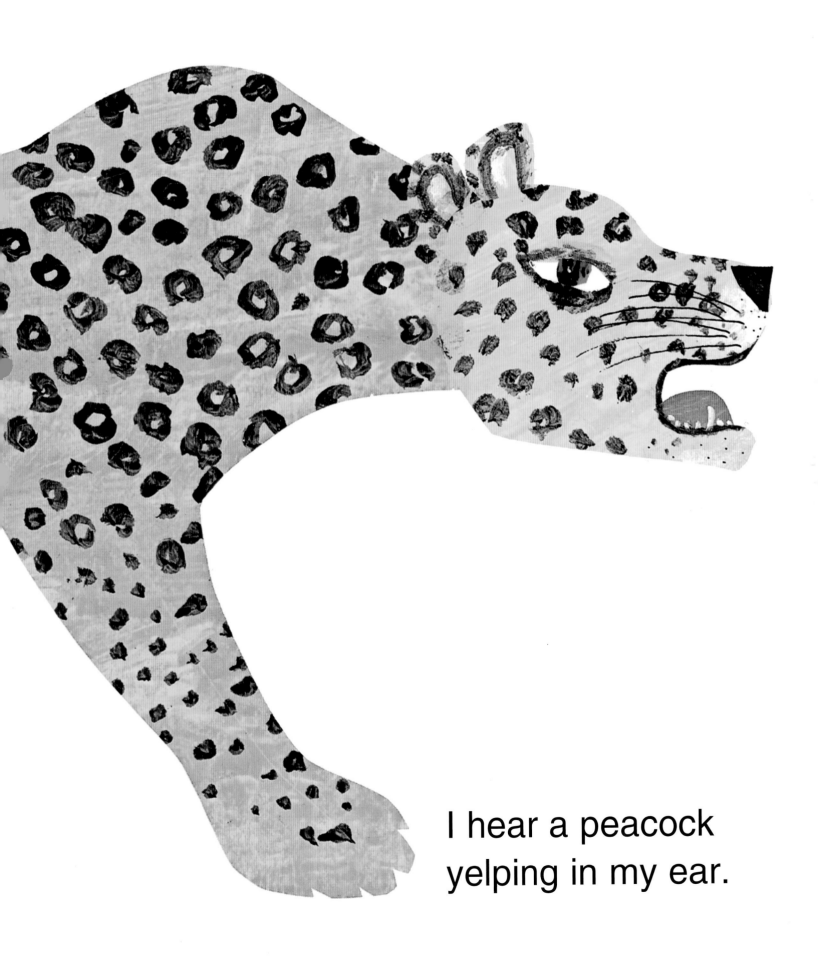

I hear a peacock
yelping in my ear.

Peacock, Peacock,
what do you hear?

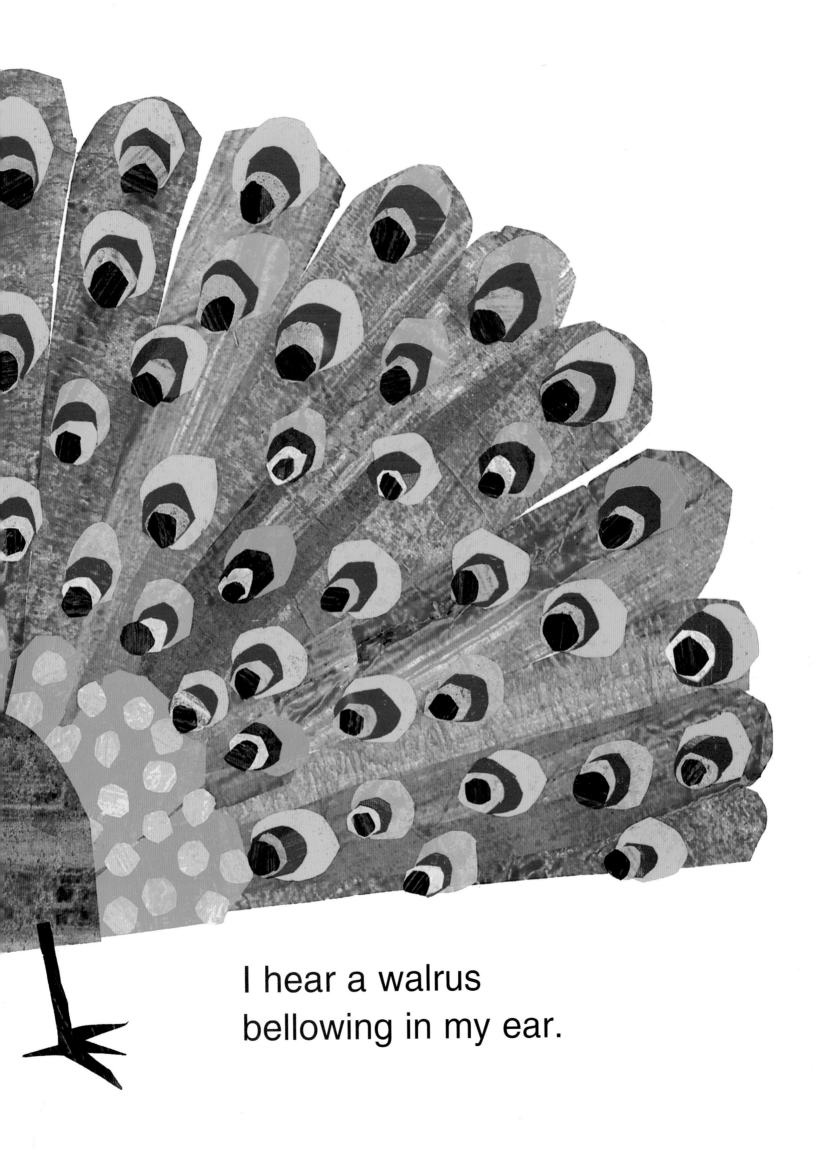

I hear a walrus
bellowing in my ear.

Walrus, Walrus,
what do you hear?

I hear a zookeeper
whistling in my ear.

Zookeeper, Zookeeper,
what do you hear?

I hear children . . .

. . . growling like a polar bear,
roaring like a lion,
snorting like a hippopotamus,
fluting like a flamingo,
braying like a zebra,
hissing like a boa constrictor,
trumpeting like an elephant,
snarling like a leopard,
yelping like a peacock,
bellowing like a walrus . . .

that's what I hear.

Place CD HERE

ERIC CARLE